Standing by Emma

JEFF GOTTESFELD

SADDLEBACK
EDUCATIONAL PUBLISHING

red rhino b**OO**ks™

With more titles on the way ...

SADDLEBACK
EDUCATIONAL PUBLISHING
www.sdlback.com

ISBN-13: 978-1-62250-920-1
ISBN-10: 1-62250-920-X
eBook: 978-1-63078-046-3

Printed in Guangzhou, China
NOR/1014/CA21401612

19 18 17 16 15   1 2 3 4 5

Emma

Age: 11

Favorite Old TV Show: *Gilmore Girls*

Best Sport: best second baseman on the school softball team

Future Goal: to be a movie costume designer

Best Quality: intelligence

CHARACTERS

Danya

Age: 12 (wishes she was 16)

Special Skill: can text faster than any kid in school

Secret Wish: spend more time with her mom

Future Goal: to be a movie makeup artist

Best Quality: loyalty

1
LOVE NOTES

Danya and Emma were best buds. They had been for a long time, even though they were very different.

Danya was tall for her age. She had long red hair. She was extra skinny. She loved her cell phone. Danya only read if she had to. And she was the class clown.

Emma was small. She had short blonde hair. She was extra fit. She loved sports. Emma was a big reader. And she was the class brain.

The girls were BFFs—best friends forever. It was like they could read each other's minds. See into each other's hearts. Everyone knew it too. All the kids in sixth grade called them "Demma." They were *that* close.

Danya had other friends, but there was no one like Emma. Danya liked boys. Boys liked her. She'd had a boyfriend. But she knew crushes didn't last. Emma would always be there for her.

Both girls lived with their moms. Danya's mom worked days. Emma's mom worked nights. They lived too far from school to walk. So Danya's mom took them in the morning. Emma's mom drove them home.

On a Monday in the fall, Emma's mom waited in her car by the school entrance.

Danya and Emma came right out when the

bell rang. They were excited. A boy named Anton had given Emma a note. Right before the bell. Emma had never had a boyfriend. But she liked Anton. He was tall, dark, and funny.

Danya knew how much Emma liked him. She had always told Emma to go and talk to Anton. But Emma never did. Until Emma got the note, Anton had never even talked to her. It was huge that he passed her a note. Scary too. It was so scary that Emma did not want to read it.

"What if he hates me?" she asked Danya.

"Boys who hate girls don't write them notes," Danya told her. She felt like she knew boys well. "Boys ignore girls they don't like. They act like the girl isn't even there."

Emma still looked worried. "What if he's the first? Maybe he sees me looking at him. Maybe he wants me to stop."

"And maybe he's inviting you to the dance." The winter dance was in three months.

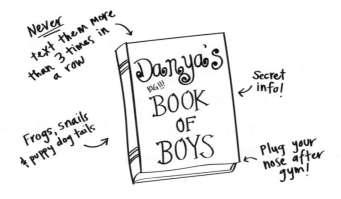

Never text them more than 3 times in a row

Danya's BIG!!! BOOK OF BOYS

Secret info!

Frogs, snails & puppy dog tails

Plug your nose after gym!

"No way!"

"How do you know unless you read it?"

"I don't want to get hurt," Emma told her. They got into the car.

"Look. Emma. If you won't read it? Give it to me. I'll read it," Danya declared. "Then I'll tell you what he said. If it's good, you can read it then."

"No!" Emma said. "Then you'll know. And I won't."

"That's crazy!" Danya yelled.

"No shouting!" Emma's mom told the girls to calm down. Her name was Rosie. That was what Danya called her. Emma called Danya's mom by her first name too.

Rosie started the car and pulled away from the curb. "What are you guys yelling about?"

"We're talking ... about a book," Danya fibbed.

"Yeah, that's right," Emma agreed. She was grinning now. "Danya says she's going to read a book. For fun. Then she's going to tell me all about it."

All three of them laughed. Rosie knew how much Danya did not like to read.

"I'll want a ten-page book report," Rosie

said. "And I am a very hard grader."

They laughed again. Rosie turned onto the road. Three lanes each way. Five minutes later, Danya felt something pushed into her hand. She looked. It was the note.

She turned to Emma. "Want me to read it? Really?"

Emma nodded.

Danya opened the note. What she read made her eyes get big.

8

2
THE CRASH

Dear Emma,

I like you. I like you a lot. You are the cutest girl in school. I can't talk when you look at me. That's why I don't sit by you at lunch. Can you come and sit by me? That would rock. Know what would rock even more? Go to the dance with me.

Love,

Anton

He had written "love." Whoa. No boy had ever used that word with Danya. The word "love" was big.

How to sign a note...

XOXO **Best Wishes** **YOUR PAL** **Love**

"So?" Emma asked. She had put her hands over her eyes.

"So, what?" Danya joked.

"What did he say?"

"What did he say about *what*?" Danya teased.

"Not funny." Emma moved her hands to look at Danya.

Danya gave her a big thumbs-up. "It's good. It's very, very good. He said he loved you."

"He loves me? He loves me?!"

Emma yelled so loud that her mom turned around.

"Whoever loves you? Keep it down!" Rosie warned. Then she went back to driving.

Emma held out her hand to Danya. "Give it to me. I want to read it."

"Nope."

"Danya. Come on."

"Come on and take it," Danya teased. "You can read how he loves, loves, loves you!"

The note was in Danya's right hand. Emma tried to take it. Danya played keep-away.

"Give it!"

Danya went to hand it to her when Rosie turned around again.

"Kids! Stop fight—"

Bam!

Danya's world went black.

A moment later, she opened her eyes.

The car had stopped. A big truck had run into them on the driver's side. The car was smashed. The air bags had popped. In the front seat, Rosie moaned.

Then Danya looked to her left. She saw Emma. Blood covered her face. Danya screamed. Her friend's eyes were closed. She was still.

Danya screamed again. Emma did not open her eyes.

Danya was sure. Her best friend was dead.

3
SIX WEEKS LATER

Emma was not dead.

Help came. Danya, Emma, and Rosie went to the ER. Danya was fine. She was sent home. Rosie stayed for two days.

Help on the way

Emma was in bad shape. There were

cuts on her face and head. Her ribs were broken. The worst was her spinal cord. Her brain could not make her legs work. After a week, she went to New York City to see expert doctors. There, maybe she could learn to walk again.

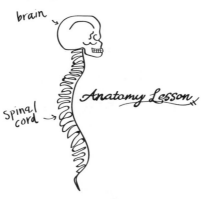

Danya did not see Emma after the crash. Rosie did not want Emma to see anyone. When Emma was in New York, Rosie said not to call. "No calls. No texts. Emma has to work on getting well."

Danya sent many cards. But the six

weeks Emma was away were hard. She kept seeing the crash in her mind. The note from Anton. The keep-away. Emma getting mad. Rosie turning. If Danya had not played keep-away …

The police were looking into the crash. There would be a full report. They had even talked to Danya. But Danya did not need to wait for their report. She already knew why it had happened. If Danya had behaved, Emma's mom would have seen the truck. There would have been no crash. Emma would fine.

Danya felt so bad. She talked about all this with her mom. Her mom had no advice. Danya had been told many times: *don't mess around in the car.* Danya swore it would never happen again. Her mom said that was good. But too late to help Emma.

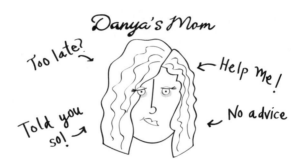

Then there were the dreams. They got so bad that Danya did not like to sleep. It was always the same. The dreams felt real. The note. The ride. The crash. In some dreams, Danya was hurt too. She woke up crying. Her mom said she needed time to get over it. Danya knew better. What she needed was Emma.

At school, there was an empty desk. In the lunchroom, Emma's seat was empty. Danya felt alone. It had been Demma for so long.

She could not wait until Emma came home from New York. But she was also afraid. What if Emma still could not walk? Would she blame Danya? Danya knew she deserved it.

One morning, Danya's mom told her they

needed to talk. They sat at the table in the kitchen.

"Rosie just called," her mom said. "Emma comes home today."

Danya was both excited and fearful. "How is she?"

Her mother shook her head. "Bad. She still can't walk."

"Oh, God." Danya started to cry.

Her mom handed her a tissue. Danya dabbed her tears.

Tissues for your Issues

"I ... I ... I need to see her," Danya declared.

"There's no rush, Danya."

"Yes there is. I have to see her. I have to say how sorry I am."

Her mom frowned. "It could be too soon."

Danya looked right in her mom's eyes. "Mom? I have to."

Her mom sighed. "Okay. I'll call Rosie. Just don't—"

"Don't what? Be surprised if she's mad at me?" Danya set her jaw. "Fine. I won't be. But I still have to see her."

Her mom got out her phone. A minute later, Danya was invited to Emma's house.

4
FACE TO FACE

Danya had not been to Emma's house since the crash. As she came up the walk, she had a teddy bear in her hands. It was brown and fuzzy. It was their thing to give teddy bears to each other. They each had many. Danya hoped Emma would like this one. If Emma was mad, maybe the bear would help. At least it was a warm day for November.

Friendship Bear

BFF

The first sign that things had changed was the ramp. There had been three steps up to Emma's porch. Now there was a ramp. Danya almost dropped the teddy bear. Her mom had said that Emma could not walk. But the ramp. Well, that made it real.

The front door opened. There was her friend. She was in a wheelchair. Her hair was super short. They must have shaved her head to sew up her cuts. She was very thin.

Rosie stepped up behind Emma. She was all smiles and energy. "Hi! Danya! It's so good to see you! I'm so glad you're here. *We're* so glad you're here. It's so good you two can see each other! Let me bring Emma out to the porch. You two can sit. Maybe talk. Maybe have some iced tea. Emma, would you like some iced tea?"

Danya tried to act normal. But it was so hard. Emma did not look the same. She stared as Rosie pushed Emma out the door and onto the porch.

"Mom, I told you. I can do it," Emma said to Rosie.

"I know, sweetie. But you know …" Rosie's voice trailed away. "Well. I'll leave you guys. And bring tea. Soon."

There was one chair and a small table on the porch. Across the street was one row of homes. Behind the homes were three hills that faced north. In winter, Danya and Emma would sled there. Sometimes the snow would last until March. In spring, they would pick wildflowers. Danya made a face. Those days were over. Emma might never sled again.

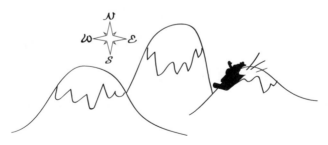

"Sit," Emma told her. "As you can see, I already am."

Danya felt the teddy bear still in her arms. "I have this. I got it for you. It's good to see you. I'm so glad you're alive." She handed the stuffed bear to Emma. Her friend took it. Looked at it. Dropped it in her lap.

"It's nice," Emma said. "Maybe you can put it on my shelf. With all the others. I can't reach it anymore. Ever."

Danya sat. Rosie came with two glasses of iced tea. Danya took one. Rosie gave the other to Emma. Then she left the girls alone.

Danya knew what she had to say. "I'm sorry, Emma. I'm so sorry. I wish I could turn back time. I wish I had just given you Anton's note."

Turn back time

1855
Too far back

3015
Too far ahead

Before the accident
just right

"What did it say?"

"Excuse me?" Danya asked.

"What did it say? I never saw the note. I don't even know what happened to it," Emma told her.

"You really want to know about the note?"

"Yup."

Danya gulped. This was not why she

came over. She had not thought about the note at all. It had stayed in the car. The car was junked. The note was long gone.

"Anton said he wanted to hang with you. He said he loved you. And he asked you to the winter dance," Danya told her evenly.

"Did he really say he loved me?"

"Yup."

Emma laughed. "Well. That's a joke. He didn't write me. Or call me. Or text me. Not once."

Danya did not know what to say to that. It was one more thing for Emma to feel bad about. So she said what she had come to say.

"Emma? I said I was sorry. Really. I have spent weeks being sorry. Do you forgive me? Do you?"

Emma stared at her. "Are you kidding? No. I don't forgive you. I won't. I can't. Look at me. If you were me, would you forgive you? No. You would not. In fact, I wish you would just go home. Take the stupid bear. I don't want it."

Emma flung the bear at Danya. It hit her and fell to the ground. Danya said nothing. She got up and walked down the ramp. Then she walked home.

5
THE BIG LIE

Danya's mom was grim. "I just talked to Emma's mom."

Danya had been on her bed. Her eyes were shut. She was thinking about Emma. She sat up. Then opened her eyes. "What did she say?"

Thinking of Emma

Her mom sat at the foot of the bed. "She said your visit upset Emma. And maybe you should not go over there again."

Danya tilted her head back sadly. "I knew it."

"She also said Emma will be back at school."

"When?" Danya asked.

"Tomorrow," her mom said. She looked sad. "This is the worst."

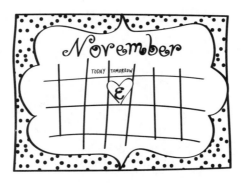

"It is," Danya moaned.

"Well. One bit of good news. Emma is not

going to blame you. She will just say the truck couldn't stop."

"That's a big lie."

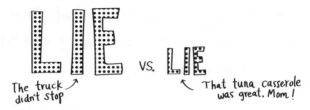

The truck → didn't stop   VS.   ← That tuna casserole was great, Mom!

Danya felt her mom touch her face gently. "It's for the best. I wish I could help you."

Danya frowned. "Why, Mom? Why? I'm getting what I deserve."

The next day was school. When she got to homeroom, Emma was there. She was in her wheelchair. She had on baggy pants and a gray shirt.

"Hey, Danya! Emma's back!" Fay Wilson called to her.

33

Danya waved. Then she waved to Emma. She hoped against hope that Emma would wave back.

She didn't. Everyone would see that Emma was ignoring her. What would they think? What would they say?

Danya checked the clock. Three minutes until class started. She put her books on her desk. Then she went to Emma. She had to try.

"Hi."

"Hi," Emma said. "My mom talked to your mom."

"Yeah. Thanks for that." Danya's hands

34

shook. She was so scared.

"What do you want?" Emma asked her.

There was a lot she wanted. But this was not the time for it. Danya had one more thing to say.

"Please. Tell me how to make it okay. I'll do anything. Anything."

Emma looked right in her eyes. "If you want to help me? Go away. And stay away."

Danya went back to her desk. The bell rang. Danya was hurt. It was a sad day. Too many bad days. Not enough good ones.

6
PARTNERS

Danya stayed away from Emma all day.

That did not mean she didn't see her. At first many kids talked to Emma. Then she was mostly alone. Danya hoped Anton would sit with her at lunch. She knew that would mean a lot. He did not even try.

Danya did not see him in the lunchroom. He ate somewhere else.

Emma was late to Ms. Reed's English class. That had been her best class. She and Danya shared a table. The teacher grinned as Emma rolled in.

"Emma! I'm so happy you're back. Sit by Danya. Your seat is saved."

Emma rolled up next to Danya. "My book bag is behind me. Can you find my book and pen? I kind of can't get them."

Danya tried to stay calm. Emma was acting normal.

"I'm here to help." She found Emma's stuff.

Ms. Reed had a project for them. They were to write a poem. It had to have five beats in the first line. Seven in the second. Five in the third. That was it. The idea was to find meaning in something simple. Ms. Reed called it a *haiku*.

"Want to do the first line?" Danya asked.

Emma nodded. "Why not? I do line one.

You do line two. I do line three."

"Yes." Danya felt good. Emma was like her old self. Maybe they were okay. Maybe all Emma needed was a normal day.

Emma picked up her blue pen. She wrote the first line fast.

Life can change like that.

"Your turn." Emma slid the paper to Danya. Danya wrote the next line.

Sometimes we let down our buds.

She handed the paper back to Emma. Emma read the second line. She smiled. Then she wrote the last line.

New buds mean new start.

The five words felt like five punches to Danya's gut.

She and Emma were not okay. They were not close to okay. Danya wondered if they would ever be okay. That poem said it all. Danya should go away. And stay away.

7
DANCE WEEKEND

Danya went away. And stayed away.
Six weeks passed. Winter came. Snow fell.

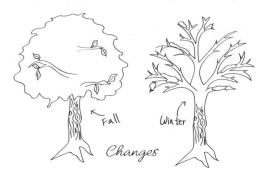

Changes

Fall   Winter

Danya and Emma did not become
Demma again. What was odd was that most
kids did not care. At first, a few kids talked

about it. Within a week, no one did. Life was like before. But there was no Demma. Sometimes it felt like there never had been a Demma.

Danya tried to smile at her ex-bud. Emma never smiled back. After a while, Danya stopped trying. She just went on with her life.

But it was not the same as before. She joked less. She cared less about boys. Three boys asked her to the winter dance. She turned them all down. She would either go alone or not at all.

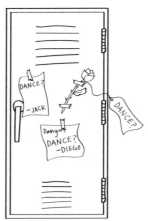

She tried to do things that mattered. There was a place downtown. It gave food to people too poor to buy their own. She worked there every weekend for three hours.

She gave two hours of time each week to the library. She did it because Emma loved books. She cleaned the bathrooms. She mopped the floors. She put books back on shelves. She even read to little kids. She thought of Emma with every turned page.

She didn't tell Emma she was doing these things. But it felt right to do them.

Do what you can... ← (get it?)

The winter dance was on a Saturday

45

night. She decided not to go. She knew no one had asked Emma to the dance.

Since Emma came back to school, Anton barely looked at her. That made Danya mad. But thinking about that made her think about Emma. She tried not to think about it.

With the dance coming, she could not ignore it. It would mean so much to Emma to be invited to the dance. She *knew* it would.

That meant she had to do something about it.

8
CHILL OUT

She knew where to find Anton. His parents owned Chill Out. It was an ice cream shop in the mall. Anton hung out there. Sometimes he cleaned tables or served ice cream. Danya got her mom to drive her to the mall.

"Where are you going?" her mom asked.

"Chill Out."

"You want an ice cream?"

Danya smiled at her mother. "Mom? Chill out. I'll be fine. It's the mall. No one is going to grab me."

Her mom grinned at her. "I know, I know. Meet me at the bookstore, then. When you're done."

"Okay. Don't worry. I'm twelve, not six. And don't say I will always be your little girl."

"Fine," her mom said. Then she winked. "You will always be my baby girl."

Danya left her mom and went to the food court. That's where Chill Out was located. The mall was quiet at this time of day. She spotted Anton at the counter. She knew he did not have a date to the dance.

"Anton!"

He turned. He had a big ice cream cone in his hand. He was such a fine boy. Tall and dark. With great hair.

The Quadruple Berry Blitz →

"Hey, Danya. Don't see you here much. Wanna ice cream?"

"Can we talk?"

"Um ... sure. I guess," he said.

"I'll get myself some. I'll be right back. Find two seats?" she said.

Anton nodded. Danya got herself a vanilla soft serve in a cup. Then she saw

Anton alone at a table. She sat with him.

"Can I ask you something?"

"Sure." He licked his ice cream.

"I'll cut to the chase. I saw the note you gave Emma. From before the crash. Why won't you talk to her? Why do you act like she isn't even alive? And why won't you ask her to the dance?"

Anton flushed. "Who are you to ask me, Danya? It's not like she's talking to *you*."

Danya held her ground. "What's going on with Emma and me? That's for her and me to discuss. Or not. But I saw your note. And don't you forget it."

He got angry. "It wasn't for you."

"Oh, stop it," Danya told him. "Emma and I were besties. We shared. Anyway, you liked her. You talked about going to the dance with her. And now? You act like she has a disease. What's your deal?"

Two other kids from school came into the shop. They looked at Danya and Anton together and grinned. Danya wanted to scream. She and Anton were not a couple. But this was not the time. She sighed. There would be a rumor. Oh well. Nothing she could do about it.

Anton kept his voice low. "Come on, Danya. You know."

"What? That she's in a wheelchair? She's the same girl. There's just some stuff she can't do. That's all." Danya waved her spoon. A blob of ice cream fell to the table.

"That's right," Anton agreed. "There's stuff she can't do. Like dance. Like sled. Like walk. Like … well, like a lot of stuff. I just don't think she's the girl for me."

Danya stood. "That's what you think matters? That a girl can't *sled*?"

But she *Can* Pop a wheelie

Anton nodded. "It may not matter to some guys. It matters to me. Hey. You don't have a date to the dance, right? Why don't we go? You and me."

52

Danya looked right at him. She could not believe what he had just said. "You want me to go to the dance with you."

"Well, yeah. I guess I do. You're hot, Danya. You have great hair. You know?"

"Because I have great hair?" Danya yelled. She was tempted to dump her ice cream on his head. Instead, she turned it over on the table in front of him.

← I wanted to do that

"Sure, Anton," she said. "I'll go with you. When that ice cream doesn't melt all over the table. I wouldn't go to the dance with

53

you if you were the last boy alive." Then she smiled. "You know? I wasn't going to go at all. But I changed my mind. I'll find the right date. And I'll see you there."

9
THE TRUTH

When Rosie opened the door, Danya was blunt. "I have to see her."

"Danya. We were just going to call—"

"Ask her in, Mom." Emma rolled into the hall. She wore gym shorts and a T-shirt. "I need to talk to her too."

Huh? Danya had been ready to beg. Instead, it was no problem.

"Well, come in, Danya," Rosie said. "We set up Emma's room on this floor now. You girls can go in there."

Emma waved to her. "Come on. Follow me."

Emma rolled toward the room that used to be the den. It was now her bedroom. Danya was behind her. She saw all the teddy bears on her bed. That made Danya happy. Emma used her arms to move from the wheelchair to her bed.

"Sit in my chair," she told Danya. "It's comfy."

Danya was wary. Emma was being so nice. It did not make sense. "Don't you want to know why I'm here?"

"Because God sent you?"

Danya laughed. "If he did, he didn't tell me."

Emma nodded. "I think a lot of the time he doesn't."

Danya sat. She pulled the wheelchair closer to Emma. "Let me tell you why I came. The winter dance is tonight."

"Ugh." Emma made a face. "Not going. Can't dance. Won't dance. Who are you going with?"

"You." Danya pointed at Emma. "With you. You're going to be my date. We are going to put on our best dresses. Then we can do each other's hair. Makeup too. Then we're going to the dance. We don't have to dance. We can sit on the side and play cards. I don't care. But I am not going to stay home alone. Neither are you. We are going. You. And me. And we are going to have fun."

Emma did a slow clap. "Nice speech. You should run for office."

"Come on. Say yes." Danya moved the wheelchair even closer.

"Anton will be there. I don't want to see him," Emma told her.

Danya folded her arms. "That is the point. I want him to see you. I want him to see that you can have fun. Because you are fun. Even if you can't dance."

"Ah." Emma picked up one of the teddy bears and held it to her heart.

"Good. Are you in?"

Emma was silent for a long time. Then she nodded. "Okay. I'm in. I'm in a wheelchair. That's true. But I'm still me. That's true too."

Whoa. Emma had said okay.

"Emma?"

"Yeah?"

"You are being nice. Do you forgive me now?" Danya looked at her. She *so* wanted her BFF back.

Emma got shy. Her cheeks turned red. "Well … my mom and me? We found out there is nothing to forgive you for."

That made no sense to Danya. She had done such a bad thing. She had ruined her best friend's life.

That's what she told Emma.

"I don't know how to say this …" Emma was so quiet Danya could barely hear her. "But it's not true. You did not ruin my life."

Danya watched as Emma burst into tears.

10
THE DANCE

Emma cried and cried. Danya just sat there. Then she put an arm around her friend. "Why the tears? What's going on?"

Puddle of tears

"Danya. Danya." Emma barely got the words out. "We got the police report. About the crash. It said the truck was going too fast. It would have hit us even if my mom had seen it. The crash wasn't your fault. Only the truck driver's."

The Accident Replay

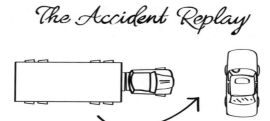

Danya sat there in shock. All these weeks she had blamed herself.

"I'm sorry," Emma said softly. "I blamed you. My mom blamed you. We blew it. So can you forgive us? Please?"

"When ... when did you find out?"

Emma hung her head in shame. "About a week ago."

Wow. A week had passed. And Emma had not said a word. All she had been to Danya was cold.

But why?

"I know." Emma put her face in her hands. "I'm so sorry. I just didn't know how to tell you."

Someone stepped into the doorway. "The same for me."

Danya looked up. Rosie was there.

"As soon as we got the report, I wanted to call your mom. But Emma wanted to tell you first. She was right," Rosie said. "I'm sorry. It was never your fault. So much happened so fast."

Danya turned back to her friend. The truth was she had done a bad thing in the car. So what if Emma had waited a week to tell her about the report? Compared to being in a wheelchair, it was nothing.

She put out her right hand. "We're good?"

Emma took her hand. "So good."

63

Danya put a second hand atop the first two. "Good. Then let's get ready. Hair, makeup, nails, and clothes. There's a lot to do."

They had a dance to get ready for.

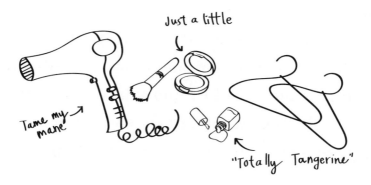

Just a little

Tame my mane

"Totally Tangerine"

Danya wore a long silver gown. Emma had on a black lace dress. The dance was in the gym. The theme was outer space.

"If this was a movie? Everyone would clap when you went in," Danya told Emma.

"I don't need clapping. I just need kids to see I'm still me."

They entered. Music played. Kids danced. And then they were face to face with Anton. Danya had told Emma what he had said at Chill Out.

"Hi," Emma said to him.

"Hi," Anton said back. "You came."

Emma nodded. "There is one good thing about being in this chair."

"What's that?" Anton asked.

"I don't have to dance with you," said Emma.

Danya grinned. "Come on, Emma. Let's hang out."

She spotted Fay and some of the other kids. They went over to them. And a great thing happened. Everything was fine. Everyone talked. Everyone had fun. They even played cards.

That was not the best thing, though. The

best thing, Danya decided, was that Demma was back. In fact, Demma was better than ever.

66